Meet the Kreeps

The Mad
Scientist

Meet the Kreeps

Meet the Kreeps

The Mad Scientist

~◈(◈)◈~

by Kiki Thorpe

Scholastic Inc.
New York • Toronto • London • Auckland • Sydney
Mexico City • New Delhi • Hong Kong • Buenos Aires

ISBN-13: 978-0-545-06561-0
ISBN-10: 0-545-06561-5

12 11 10 9 8 7 6 5 4 3 2 1   9 10 11 12 13 14/0

Printed in the U.S.A.
First printing, April 2009

For Nick

⇥ Chapter 1 ⇤

Polly Winkler stood in her room in the crumbling old mansion where she lived with her family. With her hands on her hips, she surveyed the pile of things sitting on her desk.

"Hey, Polly, let's go outside," said her best friend, Mike. He kicked a soccer ball against the wall, disturbing a spider, which scurried into a crack.

"Just a second. I want to make sure I have everything. Now, let's see. Pencils — check. Paper — check. Ruler. Notebook. Scissors. Check. Check. Check." Polly ticked them off the list in her hand. She looked around. "Where are my crayons?"

Mike looked longingly out the window. "Come on," he begged again. "This is our last chance. School starts tomorrow."

"I know," said Polly with a happy sigh. "It's going to be great!"

Mike scrunched up his nose. "What's so great about going back to school?"

"Just one thing," Polly told him. "No Kreeps."

The Kreeps were Polly's stepfamily. That summer her father had gotten remarried to a woman named Veronica Kreep, who had three children of her own. When Polly had moved into her stepfamily's home, her whole life had turned upside down. The Kreeps were the weirdest family Polly had ever met. They ate blood sausage for breakfast. They carried umbrellas on sunny days. They even had a tarantula for a pet.

But it wasn't just their habits and hobbies that made them odd. The Kreeps themselves were spooky. Esme, the littlest Kreep, bore a striking resemblance to the family cat. Damon, the middle Kreep, had a rather sinister talent for science. And Polly thought she'd once seen the oldest boy, Vincent, flying.

Then there was Veronica, Polly's stepmother. With her long black hair and her strange clothes, Veronica certainly *looked* like a witch, and Polly sometimes suspected she could do magic.

Mike was the only one who knew Polly's suspicions about the Kreeps. She'd tried to tell her older sister, Joy, and her younger brother, Petey, but they never saw the Kreeps the same way Polly did. They thought she had an overactive imagination.

After the wedding, Polly's family had moved into the Kreeps' gloomy mansion.

She'd had to get used to the dark hallways, spiderwebs, and the weird food Veronica liked to cook — not to mention her new siblings.

But now school was starting. Veronica had always homeschooled her kids, so while Polly, Petey, and Joy headed off to school, the three Kreep kids would stay at the mansion. For seven hours a day, five days a week, Polly's life would go back to being almost normal. Polly couldn't wait.

As she flopped down on her bed, a small black shadow darted from beneath it.

"Esme!" Polly cried, leaping up again. "You know you're not supposed to be in here!"

The little black cat blinked its green eyes at Polly. Then it sprinted out the door.

Polly bent down and looked under the bed. "Oh, no! She broke all my crayons —

and it was my new box for school! She's always getting into everything. Little kids are such a pain," she grumbled.

Mike stared at her. "Polly, I know you think your sister can turn into a cat —"

"Stepsister," Polly corrected him. "And I don't think it. I *know* it."

"Okay," Mike said. "But you can't go around talking like that. People will think you're nuts!"

Polly realized Mike was right. The less people knew about the Kreeps, the better. She would have to be extra-careful not to say anything about them at school.

The thought of school made Polly feel excited all over again. "Want to see what I'm wearing tomorrow?" she asked Mike.

"I want to go *outside*," he reminded her, kicking his soccer ball against the wall again.

"I'll show you what I'm wearing, and *then* we can go outside," Polly told him. "I got some new clothes, and they're really cool."

As Polly started toward her closet, she heard a deep rumble. It sounded like thunder — except that it was *in*side the house.

Mike looked around. "What was that?"

"Probably Damon," Polly said, making a face. "He's working on some experiment. He's been downstairs for days."

Polly's stepbrother Damon had a not-so-secret laboratory in the basement. He spent most of his time down there doing strange science experiments — and, more often than not, brewing up trouble.

"What experiment?" Mike asked as they heard another rumble. The noise was coming from the heating vents in the floor.

Polly shrugged. "I don't know, and I don't want to know." She held up a new pair of jeans and a bright blue shirt with the tag still on it. "See? I told you they were —"

She didn't get further. A rumble twice as loud as before cut her off. The floor beneath her feet started to shake.

Suddenly, an oily green substance sprayed up from the heating vent. It splattered all over Polly — *and* her brand-new clothes.

For a second, all Polly could do was stare at her ruined outfit. "DAMON!" she roared.

"Uh-oh," said Mike. "I think I'd better go." He scooped up his soccer ball and hurried out the door.

"That does it!" Polly snarled. She stormed out of her room and down the stairs. She was going to do something about Damon once and for all.

Polly found her stepmother in the kitchen, doing the crossword puzzle. "Hmm, what's a nine-letter word for *mother*,"

Veronica murmured, tapping her pencil to her lips. "Oh, I know . . . sorceress!"

Polly held up the ruined clothes. "Look what Damon did!" she exclaimed.

"Well, that was very nice of him," said Veronica. "Green is such a lovely color on you, Polly."

Polly scowled. "They're not *supposed* to be green," she told Veronica. "Damon made something explode and it got this . . . this *gunk* all over my new clothes!"

The green stuff had hardened into something snot-like, and was clinging to the outfit like rubber cement.

Just then, Polly's dad wandered into the room. "Dad, Damon ruined my outfit!" Polly waved the clothes at him.

Her father peered at them. "Nothing to worry about. We'll give them a few washes, and I'm sure it'll all come out," he told Polly.

8

"But I was going to wear them tomorrow! It's the first day of school!" Polly exclaimed.

"You can wear something else tomorrow," her dad said. "And you can wear them on the second day of school."

Polly couldn't believe it. Weren't her parents even going to punish Damon? "It's not fair!" she told them. "Damon never does his chores — I had to feed his salamanders the other day, you know. And now he's spoiled my new clothes, and you aren't doing anything about it."

Veronica raised her eyebrows. "Damon hasn't been feeding the salamanders?"

"Now, Polly," said her dad. "I think it's terrific that Damon has an educational hobby. Why, when I was a kid, I would get so caught up looking at my stamp collection that I sometimes forgot what time it was."

Polly frowned. What did stamps have to do with anything?

"What I'm saying, sweetie," her dad went on, "is I don't think we should get too worked up over a few harmless experiments —"

Just then, the door to the basement burst open, and Damon appeared in a puff of smoke. "Quick, Mother!" he exclaimed. "I need all the plutonium you've got!"

Polly stared. Her stepbrother was a strange sight. His pale skin looked grayish, there were circles beneath his bright green eyes, and his hair stuck out in every direction. The white lab coat he always wore was smudged with black soot.

"Why, Damon, dear," Veronica said. "We were just talking about you."

"Can't talk," Damon said, gazing wildly around the room. "I need plutonium! And an extra fire extinguisher if you've got one."

"You don't look well, Damon," Veronica remarked. "Why don't you sit down and have something to eat?"

"No time, Mother. No time! I'm on the verge of a major scientific breakthrough!" Damon began to scurry around the kitchen, opening and closing cupboards.

Veronica folded her arms. "Well, that's wonderful, darling, but Polly tells me you haven't been feeding the salamanders. And you ruined her school clothes. Her first day of school is tomorrow, you know."

Damon paused to give Polly a scornful look. "School? Who cares about school? I'm about to make scientific history! Soon the whole world will know me as the Young Einstein!"

"More like the Young Frankenstein," Polly muttered.

"Scientific history or not, you need to do your chores — *and* be considerate of your

11

sisters and brothers," Veronica told him sternly. "And what's more, I want you at dinner tonight. No more meals in the laboratory . . . Are you listening, Damon?"

"Please, Mother. Where do we keep the plutonium?" Damon opened the refrigerator.

Veronica frowned. "We don't have any plutonium."

"Gaah! Well, I need *something* radioactive!" Damon peered into the fridge and pulled out a container of moldy something-or-other. "Hmm, maybe these leftovers will work." Tucking the Tupperware underneath his arm, he scuttled from the room.

"Well!" Polly's dad said heartily. "It sounds as if he's really on to something." He wandered out of the room. A moment later, Polly heard him turn on the TV.

Veronica stood, frowning thoughtfully at the door Damon had disappeared through.

Then she turned to Polly. "You know, I think you're right. Damon has been spending too much time in his laboratory. It's time I did something about it."

Polly smiled to herself. *Ha-ha, Damon,* she thought. *You're going to get it now!*

Later that evening, the family gathered around the table for dinner. As they took their seats, one chair remained empty.

"Where's Damon?" asked Veronica.

The other kids shrugged. No one had seen Damon since that afternoon.

"I thought I told you to call your brother to dinner," Veronica said to Esme.

Polly's little stepsister was playing with a ball of green gunk from Damon's experiment. She batted it back and forth between her hands like a kitten playing with a ball of yarn. "He said he's busy," she told her mother.

"Oh, did he?" Veronica said with a dangerous frown. "We'll see about that."

Excellent! Polly thought. She wondered what Veronica was going to do. Would she ground Damon? Or take away his lab equipment? Would she forbid him from ever doing another experiment?

"You want me to call him again?" Polly asked Veronica eagerly.

"No need," said Veronica. She rubbed her hands together and clapped once. Suddenly, all the lights went out. The dining room plunged into darkness.

Polly sucked in her breath. Was it just a coincidence that the lights went out when Veronica clapped — or had Veronica *made* them go out?

As usual, Polly's dad didn't seem to notice anything strange. "Don't worry, everyone," he said, leaping up from the table. "I'll go check the fuse box."

"Let me find you a candle," Veronica said. A second later, a match flared. Veronica leaned forward, lighting the candles in the many-armed candelabras on the table. At the same moment, they heard feet pounding on the basement stairs. The door to the dining room burst open. Damon stood in the doorway, panting.

"What happened to the lights?" he gasped.

"How nice of you to join us, Damon," Veronica said pleasantly. "Won't you have a seat?"

Damon ignored her. "I'm in the middle of an important experiment. I need electricity!"

"You will not be continuing your experiment," Veronica told him, her tone becoming stern. "I have decided that you will be taking a break from your laboratory."

Damon sneered. "Please, Mother. I don't have time for jokes."

"I'm not joking," said Veronica. "I've asked you to obey a few simple rules, and you did not listen. So you've left me with no choice. As of this moment, you are forbidden from setting foot in your lab until I say so."

Damon's jaw dropped. "You can't be serious?"

"I am," said Veronica.

Polly hid her grin behind her hand. She was enjoying every moment.

"So I'm supposed to just hang around doing nothing all day?" Damon grumbled.

"Of course not," said Veronica. "I've decided to send you to school."

"School?" exclaimed Damon.

"School?" echoed Polly. This was not the punishment she'd had in mind!

Veronica nodded. "I spoke with the secretary at Endsville Elementary today. First thing tomorrow morning you'll be starting fifth grade."

"How could you do this to me, Mother?" he wailed.

How could she do this to me? Polly thought. Her weirdo mad scientist stepbrother was going to be in her class!

⊰ Chapter 2 ⊱

That night, Polly lay awake in bed, thinking about the next day of school. She imagined Damon shuffling up the school steps in his stained lab coat, while all the other school kids pointed and stared. The thought made her stomach twist into knots.

Polly rolled onto one side. And what would happen once Damon got to school? What if he used the fifth graders as guinea pigs for his latest experiment? Or — what if he turned the fifth graders *into* guinea pigs? With Damon, there was no telling what he might do.

Polly rolled onto her other side. And if Damon got into trouble at school, then people might discover the spooky truth about the Kreeps. *Maybe people won't want a family like that around,* Polly thought. *Maybe the Kreeps will have to leave town — and if they have to leave, then Dad and Petey and Joy and I will have to leave, too.*

Where would we go? Polly wondered. Wichita, where the Kreeps had come from? Or Transylvania, where their uncles and cousins lived?

Polly didn't want to move to Transylvania, and she didn't want to move to any place with "witch" in the name.

She flopped onto her back and sighed. There was no doubt about it. It was going to be a disaster. She wished she had never said anything to Veronica about Damon's experiments.

Veronica, Polly thought suddenly, sitting up in bed. *Of course!* Veronica was the one who'd decided to send Damon to school — which meant she could also un-decide. All Polly had to do was convince her stepmother that it was a bad idea. Veronica was odd, but she was smart and usually sensible. Polly was sure she would understand.

The sun had just started to peek above the horizon as Polly hopped out of bed and went in search of her stepmother. Though it was very early in the morning, Polly had a feeling she'd find her awake. Veronica was usually up all sorts of odd hours.

Sure enough, when Polly entered the kitchen, Veronica was there sipping a cup of black hawthorn tea. "Good morning, dear," she said when she saw Polly. "Or is it night? I've lost track."

Polly peered at her bloodshot eyes. "Are you okay?" she asked.

Veronica sighed. "I've just been thinking about Damon."

Polly's heart gave a leap. Maybe Veronica had already realized that he shouldn't go to school! "I was thinking about it, too," Polly said, "and I think —"

"I should have done it a long time ago, I know," Veronica finished. "I suppose I was worried he wouldn't get a good education. You hear terrible things about what they teach in schools these days. No fortune-telling, no hypnotism — it's all just reading, writing, and arithmetic. But I guess school-work isn't everything. Damon needs the chance to be around more children." She patted Polly's arm with a pale hand. "I wouldn't have realized that if it wasn't for you, Polly."

Polly shook her head. This conversation wasn't going at all like she'd planned!

Veronica's face brightened. "Well, since I was up anyway, I had time to make those."

21

She pointed proudly to a row of brown paper sacks on the counter.

"What are they?" Polly asked.

"Your lunch!" Veronica exclaimed.

Polly eyed the lumpy-looking bags. "Er . . . that's okay. I always buy lunch at school."

Veronica's face fell. "Really? Oh. What a pity. Those were the first sack lunches I ever made."

She sounded so disappointed, Polly felt a pang of guilt. With a sigh, she took a bag off the counter. "Veronica," she tried again, "I was thinking about Damon, too, and —"

"Good morning!" Polly's dad interrupted, bustling into the kitchen. He was dressed in his white dentist's coat and smelled of aftershave. "Oh, Polly, I'm glad you're up. I wanted to talk to you."

Polly looked back at Veronica, but her stepmother had turned away and was busy making a fresh pot of tea.

"I want you to do me a favor," Polly's dad said, pulling her aside.

"What is it?" Polly asked.

"Give your stepbrother a hand today. It's his first time going to school, you know. He'll need someone to show him the ropes."

Polly stared at her dad in dismay. She didn't even want be at the same school with Damon, and now she was supposed to show him around?

Polly's dad gave her a hopeful smile. She didn't want to let him down. "All right," she said unhappily.

Her dad kissed the top of her head. "Thanks, sweetheart." Suddenly, he seemed to notice Polly's clothes. "What are you still doing in your pajamas? Hurry and get ready. You don't want to be late for school!"

Polly trudged upstairs to get dressed. By the time she came back down, Joy, Vincent, and Petey were in the kitchen.

"Has anyone seen my homework?" Petey was asking.

"How could you have homework?" Vincent wondered. "It's the first day of school."

Petey shrugged. "I like to get ahead."

"Who wants a poached duck egg?" Veronica called from the stove.

For the next few minutes, the kitchen was filled with voices and the sound of cupboard doors opening and closing. Esme appeared, bouncing a ball of the sticky green gunk. It seemed to be her new favorite toy.

"Golly," said Polly's dad, checking his watch. "Look at the time. You guys had better get going if you're going to make it to school before the first bell." He looked around. "Where's Damon?"

"I'm right here," said a voice behind them.

Everyone turned to see Damon standing in the doorway. He looked as if he hadn't slept, either. The circles under his eyes were darker than ever, and his black hair stuck out in every direction. He was carrying a beat-up metal lunch box in one hand.

Veronica clasped her hands together. "Oh, darling! I can't believe it. Your first day of school!"

"*Mother.*" Damon looked embarrassed.

"Now don't you worry, pal," Dr. Winkler told him. "When you meet the kids at school, just hold out your hand and say, 'Howdy.' You'll have friends in no time."

"Sure," said Damon, not looking sure at all.

"I want to go to school, Mummy," said Esme, tugging her mother's skirt and getting it sticky with green gunk.

"Not until next year, dear," Veronica told her.

Phew! Polly thought. She was glad Veronica wasn't sending Esme to school, too. One Kreep at Endsville Elementary was more than enough.

"Come on," Polly said to Damon and Petey. "We'd better get going, or we'll be late."

Veronica kissed Damon's cheek. She followed the three kids to the front door. "Are you sure you have everything?" she asked Damon. "Oh, I almost forgot! Your lunch!"

"It's all right, Mother," Damon said over his shoulder. "I packed my own."

Veronica dabbed at her wet eyes. She stood on the doorstep, waving as they headed down the street.

As soon as they were out of sight, Polly stopped and turned to Damon. It was time to take matters into her own hands.

"Okay, let's get a few things straight," she said. "If you're going to be in fifth grade, you have to start acting like a fifth grader. You can't go to school dressed like that."

"Like what?" Damon asked.

"In that messy old lab coat," Polly said. "You look like you're dressed up for Halloween."

"But if I don't wear a lab coat, how will people know I'm a scientist?" asked Damon.

Polly sighed. "You're not supposed to be a scientist in the fifth grade, Damon. You're just supposed to be a kid."

Damon seemed to give that some thought. Then he took off his coat. Underneath, he was wearing jeans and a black T-shirt.

"Goggles, too," said Polly.

Damon removed the safety goggles from his forehead.

Better! thought Polly. Damon looked almost normal. Maybe this wouldn't be so bad after all.

"One more thing. Ditch the lunch box," she advised Damon. "No one has a lunch box in fifth grade."

"It's not a lunch box," Damon said. He started to hurry down the sidewalk.

Polly chased after him. "Wait a minute. Why are you in such a rush? And what's in the box?"

"Nothing." Damon kept walking.

Polly started to get a bad feeling. "Damon, you had better show me what's in that box, or I'm telling Veronica that you've been sneaking chocolate-covered ants from the pantry between meals."

"Fine." Damon stopped and opened the lunch box. Inside was a strange-looking contraption. It had a rubber wheel attached to a crank handle and wires going in every direction.

"What is it?" Polly asked.

"An electrostatic capacitor," said Damon, seeming very pleased. "I made it myself. You see, I just turn the handle," he cranked it a few times, "and it generates an electrical charge." The air around the box crackled with electricity.

"What's it for?" Polly asked.

Damon reached down and touched a dandelion growing from the sidewalk. It exploded in a burst of fluff. Polly gasped.

Damon raised his eyebrows. "Have you ever heard of spontaneous human combustion?"

"I don't think so," Polly said nervously. She didn't like where this was going.

"It's when a person suddenly bursts into flames," Damon explained. "No one knows why it happens. But there are theories. Some believe it's caused by static electricity. I plan to test that theory at school today.

"You see," Damon added with an evil smile, "if I can't be in my own lab, I'll make the *school* my laboratory!" He shut the lunch box with a snap, then shuffled off down the sidewalk, chuckling.

"Better hurry, Polly," he called back over his shoulder. "I'd hate to be late on the first day of class!"

Polly stared after him in horror. She'd been wrong. This wasn't going to be as bad as she thought — it was going to be much, much worse!

⚛ Chapter 3 ⚛

As they got closer to school, Polly found herself walking slower and slower. Soon she lagged far behind Damon and Petey. She was dreading the moment when the first bell would ring.

Mike was waiting for Polly at their usual spot near the flagpole. When he saw Damon, his eyes opened wide. "What's *he* doing here?"

"Going to school," Polly replied unhappily. "And he's going to be in our class."

"Wow!" Mike said. "This is going to be weird."

"It's going to be a disaster!" said Polly.

"So what are you going to do?" asked Mike.

Polly shook her head. "I don't know. Do you think it's too late for me to transfer to another school?"

Just then, someone called Polly's name in a singsong voice. She turned and saw Denise Dunleavy making her way toward her.

Polly groaned inwardly. Denise was in Polly's class, but they weren't friends. Denise spent a lot of time talking about how great she was, and how *un*-great everyone else was. She had a way of making Polly feel about two inches tall.

"Well, I see you haven't changed at all since last year," Denise said, looking Polly over. "*I* grew an inch and a half, and I got a whole new wardrobe. Do you like my outfit? It cost over a hundred dollars." She stepped back so that Polly could admire her white jeans and pink polka-dot shirt.

Behind Denise's back, Mike made a face. He didn't like Denise, either.

"I went on a cruise with my parents," Denise continued. "It was so great. The cruise ship had three pools and a movie theater. I wish I could have stayed there forever."

"Too bad you didn't," Mike mumbled.

"So what did *you* do this summer?" Denise asked Polly.

"Er . . ." Polly wasn't sure what to say. She didn't want to tell Denise about the Kreeps becoming her family. Denise had thought Polly's family was weird even before Polly's dad had married Veronica.

Luckily, Mike changed the subject. "Is that your breakfast?" he asked, pointing to the paper cup and jelly doughnut Denise was holding. "You drink coffee?"

"Of course not," said Denise. "Coffee stunts your growth, and I need to be tall when I'm older because I'm going to be a model. This is for our teacher. I thought it would be nice to bring him breakfast on the first day of school."

Polly gritted her teeth. She knew that Denise was bringing their teacher breakfast so that she would be his favorite. Denise always wanted to be teacher's pet.

Denise glanced past Polly and wrinkled her nose. "Who is *that*?"

Polly turned and saw Damon making his way over to them.

"Look at his hair." Denise snickered. "Doesn't his mother make him comb it?"

Damon smiled as he walked up to them. "Howdy." He held out his hand to Denise, just as Polly's dad had told him to do. "I'm Damon."

Polly took a deep breath. "Damon is my —"

But she didn't get any further. As Damon reached for Denise's hand, there was an electric crackle, then — *Sploosh!*

The jelly doughnut exploded.

Denise spluttered in surprise. Strawberry jelly was splattered all over her clothes as well as Damon's electrostatic capacitor.

"Curses!" Damon jiggled the handle. "Your cholesterol-laden breakfast pastry has jammed the gears!" He shuffled away, mumbling to himself.

"He ruined my outfit!" Denise wailed.

"At least the jelly matches the polka dots on your shirt," Mike said.

Denise glared at Mike and stormed away. As she strode into the school, kids pointed at her and laughed.

Mike turned to Polly and grinned. "At

least you aren't the only one whose clothes got ruined."

But Polly didn't feel better. She had a feeling that the trouble was just beginning.

A short time later, Polly, Mike, and Damon were all seated in their new classroom.

"Welcome to the fifth grade," their teacher said. "I'm Mr. Crane."

Mr. Crane was tall and thin. He had a beard like Abraham Lincoln and a friendly smile.

"He seems cool," Mike whispered to Polly.

Polly nodded. *I just hope Damon doesn't mess everything up,* she thought.

She glanced over at Damon. He was sitting quietly with his hands folded on his desk, as if he had been going to school all his life. So far, so good.

Just then Denise hurried in. Her clothes were smeared with pink stains where she'd wiped off the jelly. As she slunk into her seat, she gave Damon a poisonous look.

Mr. Crane went on, "We have a few new students in the class this year. So I thought we could start by going around and saying something about ourselves."

As the other kids took turns telling about their summer vacations and their favorite video games, Polly chewed her lip nervously. She was worried about what Damon would say. Would he tell the class that he spent his summer doing freaky experiments in the basement? Would he brag about his sinister creations? Would Damon know better than to share his spooky secrets with the class?

Polly doubted it.

By the time it was Damon's turn,

Polly's heart was hammering in her chest. Damon stood up from his chair. "I'm Damon Kreep."

"He's a creep, all right," Denise sneered. The kids around her snickered.

"Go on, Damon," Mr. Crane said. "Tell us something about yourself."

"I am a scientist," said Damon, with a proud lift of his chin.

Mr. Crane's face lit up. "Well, you're in luck, Damon. We'll do some really fun science stuff in class this year."

"You mean like cloning ourselves?" Damon asked hopefully.

Mr. Crane blinked. "Er, no. More like studying the solar system."

"Oh." Damon sounded disappointed. "I was hoping for something with a little more bang."

As he sat back down in his chair, he reached toward the boy in front of him.

Polly's eyes widened. He was going to zap that kid! "STOP!" she shrieked, leaping up from her desk.

Everyone turned to her, startled. The teacher raised his eyebrows. "Is something the matter?"

"It's — he —" Polly stuttered. She pointed to Damon's hand.

Damon looked down. Suddenly, Polly realized he was holding a pencil. He handed it to the boy in front of him. "You dropped this," he said.

All the kids were still staring at Polly. As she sat back down, feeling foolish, she heard the girl behind her whisper, "Polly is so weird."

"Yeah, but that new boy is kind of cute, don't you think?" the girl's friend whispered back.

"Yeah, he has cool hair," the first girl whispered. "He looks just like a rock star."

Damon? Cute? Polly was stunned. One thing was for sure, the first day of school was not turning out at all like she expected!

The rest of the morning, Mr. Crane had them organize their supplies in their desks and do an art project to decorate the bulletin boards. It should have been a fun morning, but Polly was too worried to enjoy herself. At any moment, she expected Damon to pull some mad scientist stunt.

By the time the bell finally rang for lunch, Polly couldn't wait to get out of the classroom. She jumped up from her desk and joined the line of students filing toward the cafeteria.

"What's Damon doing?" Mike asked as they shuffled forward in the line.

Polly looked around. Damon was headed down the hall in the other direction.

"Damon!" Polly chased after him. "Where are you going? Lunch is this way."

"I'm not hungry," Damon said. "I'm going to find the laboratory."

"There *is* no lab," Polly told him. "And you can't just walk around the halls by yourself. There are rules about that!"

"Gaah!" Damon stamped his foot in frustration. "What kind of school doesn't have a lab?"

"It's called a grade school," Polly said, steering him toward the cafeteria. "And you'd better get used to it."

By the time Polly got to the lunch-room, her stomach was growling. She took a seat at the fifth-grade table and opened the lunch Veronica had made. As she pulled out a sandwich, a powerful odor filled the air.

"What's that smell?" asked Denise, who was sitting across from her. "It stinks!"

The stench seemed to be coming from Polly's sandwich. Cautiously, she peeled back the top. A row of smelly, silver sardines stared up at her from the bread.

"Ew!" Denise squealed, loud enough for everyone at their table to hear. "That's the grossest sandwich I've ever seen!"

Embarrassed, Polly shoved the sandwich back in the paper bag. She took out a hard-boiled egg and tapped it against the table to break the shell.

Splat! Slimy goop spurted into her hand. The egg was raw!

Denise and her friends shrieked with laughter. Polly tried to ignore them. As she wiped her hand on her napkin, her stomach grumbled again. *There has to be something in here that I can eat,* she thought. *There was an apple, wasn't there?*

Yes, Polly felt something firm and round. She pulled it out of the bag, and her heart sank.

It wasn't an apple. It was an onion.

That's Veronica's idea of lunch? Polly fumed. *A sardine sandwich, a raw egg, and an onion?*

Denise made a face and put down her own sandwich. "I can't eat anymore," she announced. "Polly's weird lunch made me lose my appetite."

Plugging their noses, Denise and her friends got up from the table. Polly angrily crumpled up her lunch bag and pushed it away. The Kreeps didn't even need to be there to ruin her first day of school.

"Here." Mike handed her half of his peanut butter and jelly sandwich. Polly gratefully took it. Thank goodness she had Mike as a friend.

On Polly's other side, Damon was busy

unpacking his own lunch. He took out two bottles of red soda. As he twisted the cap off one, the boys sitting across from him watched curiously.

"That's all you have for lunch? Soda?" asked a boy named Brad.

"You must have the awesomest mom in the world," added his friend Tad.

Polly was surprised. Brad and Tad were two of the most popular boys in the fifth grade. They didn't talk to just anyone.

"What kind of soda is it?" Brad asked, examining a bottle. "There's no label."

Polly knew the soda was Damon's special recipe. He had made it for their parents' wedding and served it in place of the punch. It caused terrible burping in anyone who drank it.

But Damon simply smiled as if Brad's question was just the one he'd been waiting for. "Try some," he said, holding out the bottle.

"No!" Polly shouted over to Brad. "You don't want to —"

Too late! The boy took a big swig of soda. As he set down the bottle, a funny look crossed his face.

"Oh, no!" Polly whispered to Mike. Damon had just poisoned the most popular kid in class!

Brad frowned and rubbed his stomach. Then he opened his mouth and —

B U R P!

The sound echoed through the lunchroom. Damon cackled and rubbed his hands together.

"Whoa!" Brad blinked and shook his head. "Dude, that was . . ."

"Yes?" Damon leaned forward eagerly. Polly put her head in her hands.

". . . the awesomest soda I have ever had!" Brad finished.

"Huh?" Polly, Mike, and Damon all looked at him in surprise.

"Let me try!" Tad grabbed the bottle and swallowed a gulp. He let out an even louder burp. The lunchroom monitor looked over at them and scowled.

"Outrageous!" The two boys slapped a high five.

"I'm Brad," the red-haired boy told Damon.

"I'm Tad," said his friend. "Where did you get this soda?"

"I made it," Damon replied.

"Dude, that's awesome!" said Tad. He grabbed the bottle. "We have to take this out to recess. I want to see if I can burp the whole alphabet!"

The three boys got up from the table and headed out to the playground. Polly stared after them in amazement. She couldn't believe it. Her strange stepbrother had just made friends with two of the coolest boys in the class!

"Come on," she said to Mike. "We'd better follow them."

She started to get up from the table, only to find the lunchroom monitor looming over her. "Is that your mess?" the woman asked, pointing to the raw egg dripping from the table.

"Yes," Polly said sheepishly. "But —"

"Clean it up," the monitor ordered. "And while you're at it, you can wipe down the rest of the table, too. Maybe that will teach you not to make a mess." She slapped a damp rag down on the table, then stood back and folded her arms.

Polly sighed and picked up the smelly rag. *If this is what fifth grade is like,* she thought, *it's going to be a long year.*

❧ Chapter 4 ❧

Over the next few days, Polly kept a close eye on Damon. She was sure that he was going to do something awful.

But as it turned out, Damon wasn't the one getting into trouble at school. Polly was.

Once, Polly noticed that Damon was gone with the bathroom pass for an *awfully* long time. As soon as Polly got the chance, she snuck into the boys' bathroom to see what he'd been up to. Unfortunately, all she found there was Mr. Mopp, the janitor, fixing a sink. Polly got in trouble and had to miss recess for the rest of the day.

Another time, Polly was sure she saw Damon feeding Freddie, the class hamster, something other than hamster pellets. When she tried to prove it, Polly accidentally let Freddie out of his cage. He got behind the radiator, and it took all of social studies period to get him out. Polly had to stay after school for that one.

Then one day at recess, Polly saw Damon doing a science experiment for a group of first graders. They watched, wide-eyed, as Damon dropped something into a vial of liquid, which started to hiss and bubble.

Polly gasped. "What's he doing to those little kids?"

She raced over and shoved the first graders out of the way. She was sure she'd saved them, but unfortunately, the playground monitor didn't see it that way. He sent Polly to the principal's office for pushing kids around.

"I don't understand it," Ms. Stern, the principal, said to Polly. "You've never had trouble in school before."

"I never had to go to school with Damon before," Polly grumbled.

"Damon Kreep?" Ms. Stern asked in surprise. "But he isn't any trouble at all. In fact, he's a model student. I hear he's very popular, too."

Polly gritted her teeth. Now even the principal thought Damon was great. Since the first day of school, when he'd won over Brad and Tad, Damon had made even more friends. The boys all thought he was funny and the girls thought he was cute. Even Mr. Crane seemed to like Damon. As soon as Freddie was rescued from the radiator, he put Damon in charge of feeding him.

"I don't get it," Mike said when Polly complained to him. "I thought you wanted

50

people to like Damon. Aren't you glad they don't think he's weird?"

"Yeah, but . . ." How could she explain? Polly didn't want her stepbrother to be weird. But she didn't want him to be Mr. Popular, either.

The only person who *didn't* seem to like Damon was Denise. She had never gotten over what he'd done to her clothes on the first day of school.

And then one day, Denise got her revenge.

It was the second week of school. The class was busy with a spelling worksheet, and Mr. Crane was out of the room. Damon got up to sharpen his pencil — he took one step and fell flat on his face.

The class burst into laughter. Damon's face turned pink. He tried to scramble to his feet and ended up belly flopping again.

The class laughed even harder. Finally, Damon discovered the problem: His shoelaces were tied to the desk leg.

"Wha —?" he stuttered. "But how —?"

"How was your *trip*, Damon?" Denise sneered.

"What are you talking about?" Damon snapped, trying to untangle himself from the chair. "I haven't been anywhere."

The class howled. Polly shook her head. Damon might have been a science genius, but when it came to being a fifth grader he was still pretty clueless.

Eventually, Damon untangled his shoelaces. But for the rest of the day, the class wouldn't let him forget it. "How was your *trip*, Damon?" they teased him. "Hey, Damon, have a good *fall*?"

With each joke, Damon grew more furious. He walked around looking as if there was a storm cloud over his head.

That afternoon, Mr. Crane made an announcement. "The school science fair is coming up," he said. "And I hope you'll all participate. This is a chance for everyone to have some fun with science."

Polly sat up straighter. She always liked the science fair. It was held in the school gym. Practically everyone in the school showed up to see all the different projects.

"Your project can be anything," Mr. Crane went on. "It can be a research project or an experiment or something you've invented, just so long as it has to do with science. The first-place project will go on to the state science fair, which is a lot of fun."

He held up a stack of papers. "These are your entry forms. Don't lose them! Anyone who wants to be in the science fair *must* hand in a form to me by the day before the fair. Now, you don't have to be in the science fair. But you should all try to help each other with your projects and get each other to participate. If every one of you enters, then I'll throw the class an ice-cream party."

The class murmured with excitement.

As Mr. Crane passed out the forms, Polly glanced over at Damon. He didn't look angry anymore. He was hunched down in his seat, rubbing his hands together and grinning.

Polly didn't like the look of that grin. She didn't like it at all.

"So what's new in the fifth grade?" Polly's dad asked at dinner that night.

Polly poked at something green and

slimy on her plate. "The school science fair is next week," she began, "and —"

"The science fair!" her dad exclaimed heartily. He turned to Damon. "Well, son, that's right up your alley! What are you doing for your project?"

"I can't tell you," Damon replied.

"Ooh! I know!" Joy piped up. "You should try turning a butterfly into a caterpillar!" Her forehead wrinkled. "Or is it the other way around?"

"I have a better idea. Why don't you try turning Joy from a cheerleader into a human being," Vincent said with a smirk.

"How about a project on what makes some people good at spelling?" suggested Petey, who happened to be a spelling champion.

"No, make it about spiders!" chimed in Esme, who loved creepy, crawling things.

Damon waved away their ideas. "I actually had something else in mind," he said.

Polly jabbed her fork into her dinner so hard that it slithered off her plate. *Why is everyone so interested in Damon's project?* she fumed. *Why doesn't someone ask me what I'm doing?*

"There's just one thing," Damon said with a sideways glance at his mother. "For my project, I'll need to get into my lab . . ."

Polly's fork clattered to her plate. "No fair! Damon is supposed to be grounded from his lab!" she exclaimed.

"Well," said Polly's dad, glancing at Veronica. "I'm sure we could let him use it, just this once. Don't you think so, dear?"

Veronica furrowed her brow. "I suppose it would be all right, just this once. Since it is a project for school."

"Excellent." Damon had hopped up from the table and was already heading for the door.

"But it's not fair!" Polly said again. "Why should Damon get to use his lab? I'm doing a science project, too!"

"That's a good point," said Polly's dad. "I have an idea. Why don't you and Damon work in his lab together?"

"*Together*?" Polly and Damon looked at each other in disgust.

"That's a wonderful idea!" Veronica chimed in. "Come on, both of you. I'll unlock the lab for you now."

"Go on, Polly," her dad urged.

Polly reluctantly got up from the table. The last thing she wanted was to be stuck in the lab with the mad scientist himself.

But as she followed Veronica down to the

basement, she started to change her mind. Damon knew a lot about science. He might really be able to help her with her project. And this way Polly could keep an eye on what Damon was doing. Maybe it wasn't such a bad idea after all.

⚜ **Chapter 5** ⚜

Ah, home, sweet home!" Damon said as he entered his lab. He took a deep breath of the musty air.

"Have fun, you two," said Veronica, shutting the door behind them.

As soon as his mother was gone, a mischievous look crossed Damon's face. He scuttled over to his worktable.

"Look at all this stuff." Polly examined an odd piece of equipment that bristled with tubes and levers. Lab mice skittered in their cages. A skeleton stood in the corner, its jaw hanging open as if it was surprised by everything it saw.

59

Polly picked up a giant moth pinned inside a glass box. "Wow, that's a big bug!"

"Don't touch that!" Damon snapped. "Don't touch *anything*." He was pulling bottles and jars from a nearby cabinet.

Polly put down the moth and went over to him. "So what are we going to do?"

Damon didn't answer. He was busy pouring clear liquid into a test tube.

Polly watched him curiously. "What is that?"

"You'll see," said Damon. He took a spoonful of powdered crystals and dumped them into the test tube. Then he added a drop of something from a bottle. The liquid turned yellow.

"Cool!" Polly's eyes widened.

Damon added a drop from a different bottle. The liquid turned green.

"Ooh!" Polly gasped.

Damon picked up a wooden stick and gave his creation a few stirs. Then he handed it to Polly. "There you go!" he said.

"But what is it? What am I supposed to do with it?" Polly asked, as Damon took her by the shoulders and hustled her toward the door.

"Water, sugar, and food coloring. Stick it in the freezer for three hours. Then take it out and eat it." He shoved Polly out of the lab and slammed the door behind her.

For a moment, Polly stood there, stunned. She couldn't believe it. Damon had tricked her — by making *a Popsicle*!

"Hey!" She banged on the door. "Let me in! We're supposed to be working together, Damon!"

The door opened a crack. "I'd rather eat Protozoa. Go off and do your stupid little

project, and let the real genius get to work."
He shut the door in her face.

"You think you're so great!" Polly yelled
at the door. "Well, I'll show you, Damon. I'll
make a science project better than yours!"

"I'd like to see you try!" came Damon's
muffled voice.

Polly stormed away from the lab. *I will,*
she thought angrily. *I'll show Damon. I'll
show them all!*

Later that evening, Polly sat in her
room, trying to come up with her science
project. She took out a pencil and notebook so she could write down her ideas. She
sat for a long time looking at the blank
paper.

Mr. Crane had told the class that if
they were having trouble thinking of a

project, they should start with a question. Something they'd always wondered about. "Being a scientist is a lot like being a detective," he'd said. "You follow the clues until you think you have an answer."

Polly wrote down the first question that popped into her head: *Why is Damon such a jerk?*

It was a good question. But try as she might, Polly couldn't think of a scientific way to prove the answer.

Polly wrote down her next question: *What was that slimy, green stuff at dinner tonight?*

She tapped her pencil against the paper. She *could* think of how to get to the bottom of that one. But she wasn't sure she wanted to.

And besides, she needed something more exciting. Her science project had to be so spectacular that everyone would forget Damon's science project even existed!

Polly chewed her eraser. Just what *was* Damon's project, anyway?

Suddenly, she noticed the house was strangely quiet. There were no sounds coming from the basement. No explosions rattling the windows. No clouds of smoke drifting up through the vents.

Polly went over to a small closet in the hallway. Inside was a laundry chute that led right to the basement. She stuck her head into the closet and listened.

Silence.

Polly went back to her room and sat down at her desk. She tried to think more about her science project. But she couldn't concentrate. Her mind kept wandering back to Damon.

Finally, she snapped her notebook shut.

She had to know what her stepbrother was doing.

The house was quiet as Polly crept back down to the basement. When she got to the lab, she tried the handle. It was locked. She could hear Damon shuffling around inside.

At the bottom of the door was a large gap where the door didn't quite meet the floor. Light spilled from it. Polly kneeled down and peeked through. She saw Damon's sneakers pacing back and forth across the room. He was muttering to himself.

Suddenly, he stopped in his tracks. "I've got it! It's brilliant. Soon they will all be sorry they ever made fun of Damon Kreep. Ha-ha-ha!"

A gasp escaped Polly's throat. She clamped a hand over her mouth, but it was too late. Damon's feet swiveled and moved quickly to the door.

"Who's there?" he demanded.

Polly scrambled back and ducked into the shadows.

Damon yanked open the door. "Esme, is that you?" he asked, peering out into the darkness. "I *told* you, stay out of my lab!"

He slammed the door. As soon as Polly heard the lock click, she turned and fled for the stairs. There was no doubt about it now. Damon was up to something truly evil!

Polly had to find out what he was doing for his science project. She needed to get into the lab when Damon wasn't there. The fate of the school — and maybe even the world — depended on it!

❧ Chapter 6 ❧

"Y ou want me to do *what*?" Mike asked.

"Come on, Mike. I really need your help," Polly told him.

The two friends were walking home from school. It was a few days after Polly had been to Damon's lab, and she had finally come up with a plan.

"Won't Damon mind if he finds out we went into his lab?" asked Mike.

"Of course he'll mind! That's why we have to be sneaky," Polly told him. "He's hanging out with Brad and Tad today. Now is the perfect time. Who knows when I'll get another chance?"

They had reached Polly's house. Mike looked up at the gloomy old mansion and shivered. "I'm not sure I want to go into the basement."

"You don't even have to go into the house. You can stand right here in the flowerbed."

"With the Venus flytraps?" Mike asked, eyeing the giant plants that grew there. They had leaves the size of footballs. Veronica had planted the monstrous flytraps when she moved in. Polly hardly even noticed them anymore.

"They don't bite," she told Mike. "At least, not that I know of."

Mike shivered again.

"Now, if my calculations are right, this window should lead to Damon's lab." Polly pointed to a dark cellar window. "While I sneak in through the window, you'll stay on the lookout for Damon."

"Why don't you just use the door?" Mike asked.

"Damon locked it. He doesn't want anyone to know what he's up to." Since her last visit, Polly had made another secret trip to the lab. She'd discovered the door bolted, just as she suspected it would be. "Now, we'll need some kind of signal," she told Mike. "That way I'll know he's coming."

"How about a whistle?" Mike suggested.

Polly nodded. "That's good. After Damon goes into the house, I figure I'll have three minutes to get out of his lab."

"What if someone asks what I'm doing in the flowerbed?" said Mike.

Polly shrugged. "Make something up. Ready?"

Mike nodded.

Polly tugged on the cellar window, which

opened with a squeak. She climbed down inside.

As she lowered herself into the basement, her foot brushed against something. Polly glanced over her shoulder, but it was too dark to see anything. She wiggled down until she was hanging from the window ledge, but she still couldn't reach the floor. She was going to have to drop.

Polly let go. She hit the floor and stumbled backward. A second later, something landed on top of her. Bony fingers brushed her arms.

Polly screamed.

"Are you all right?" Mike's face appeared in the window.

"Yeah." Polly climbed to her feet and picked up the skeleton she'd knocked over. Carefully, she stood it back in its corner.

Polly flicked on her flashlight and turned to the rest of the lab. It looked different without Damon there. The Bunsen burners were cold. Vials of liquid were lined up neatly in a rack. Polly took the cork off one and sniffed it.

"Yuck!" It smelled like rotten eggs. She stuck the cork back in and returned it to the rack.

Polly moved over to a row of jars against one wall. Gray, fleshy things floated inside them like pickles. One looked like a lizard with wings. Another looked like a four-headed worm.

Polly shuddered. *Any one of those gross things would make a good science project*, she thought. But she knew Damon wouldn't settle for a pickled lizard. His project would be bigger — and scarier.

An old chalkboard leaned against the wall. Something on it caught Polly's eye. She looked closer. It was a chalk drawing of the school gymnasium. Lots of little stick figures filled the gym, like people in a crowd.

At the bottom, in Damon's messy handwriting, it read *They will all be my slaves!*

The words made Polly's blood run cold. What on earth was Damon up to?

Just then, she heard keys jingle in the lock. Damon was back! But how had he gotten in without Mike seeing him?

She didn't have time to think about it. Quickly, she hid behind the mice cages.

And not a moment too soon. A second later, Damon walked in. "Laugh at me, will they?" he muttered to himself. "Well, they won't be laughing for long. Once I hit them with my remote mind-control device, those fools will all be answering to me!"

Polly's eyes widened. So that was it! Damon had a mind-control device — and he was going to bring it to the school science fair!

"Now," said Damon, "to test out my creation." He started toward the mouse cages. Polly shrank back. She was going to be caught!

But at that moment, she heard a faint call from upstairs. Damon stopped in his tracks. He scowled and yelled out, "I'm busy, Mother!"

Polly couldn't hear Veronica's reply, but it must have been stern. Grumbling, Damon left the room, locking the door behind him.

Polly leaped out from behind the cages and scrambled out the window.

Outside, she grabbed Mike. "Come on!" she exclaimed. "Let's get out of here!"

They raced away from the house. When they were a block away, Polly slowed to a stop.

"What happened?" she shouted at Mike. "You were supposed to send a signal! Damon almost caught me snooping in his lab!"

"Oops." Mike shrugged. "Sorry, Polly. I guess I forgot. Veronica came by, and we starting talking about the Venus flytraps. Did you know they eat their prey *alive*? They're so cool. I asked her if she'd let me have one so I can —"

"Who cares about Venus flytraps?" Polly interrupted. "I was almost toast in there!"

Mike looked startled. "Geez, stop shouting. What's the big deal, anyway?"

"What's the big deal? The big deal is that while you were *gardening* with Veronica, I was in terrible danger!"

"What are you talking about?" Mike asked.

"Damon has a mind-control device. He's going to use it to enslave the whole school!" Polly told him breathlessly.

Mike shook his head. "That's crazy, Polly."

"It's not crazy," Polly shot back. "I heard him talking about it! He can't be in the science fair, Mike. If he wins, he'll go to the state science fair, and who knows what will happen then! We have to stop him!"

"You know what I think?" Mike said slowly. "I think you're just jealous."

Polly was stunned. "Jealous? Of Damon? Are you kidding? He's a total weirdo!"

But Mike went on, "You're jealous and you want to mess up his project so he won't win the science fair. Well, that's cheating. I'm not going to help you."

He turned on his heel and walked away.

"Mike, wait," Polly called after him. "I'm sorry I yelled at you. But you have to help me!"

Mike just shook his head and kept walking.

Polly's heart sank. If Mike wouldn't help

her, who would? Not her dad or Veronica. Not Mr. Crane or the other kids at school.

Polly could only think of one person who could help her, one person who would want to keep Damon out of the science fair.

She was going to have to talk to Denise.

❖ Chapter 7 ❖

S o," said Denise the next morning, "you want to keep Damon out of the science fair."

"Right." Polly nodded. It was recess, and the two girls were huddled in a corner of the schoolyard, talking.

Denise narrowed her eyes. "Why does it matter to you if he's in the science fair or not?"

Polly hesitated, then shrugged. She didn't want Denise to know the truth about Damon — or the Kreeps.

"Oh, I get it," said Denise. "You're afraid he's going to beat you, and you're jealous."

"I am not!" Polly exclaimed. "Anyway," she added quickly, "are you going to help me or what?"

"It will drive Damon crazy not to be in the science fair. I love it!" Denise said with a wicked grin. Then she frowned. "On the other hand, if Damon isn't in the science fair, then we don't get to have a class ice-cream party."

Denise twirled a curl around one finger thoughtfully. "Hmm, which is better? Helping you? Or eating ice cream?"

"I'll buy you ice cream!" Polly blurted desperately.

Denise nodded. "Every day for a week. And I get to pick out anything I want."

Polly swallowed hard. Buying Denise ice cream every day would take all of her allowance. But what other choice did she have? "All right," she agreed. "So what should we do?"

"Well," Denise leaned in closer, "Mr. Crane said that you have to turn in an entry form to be in the science fair, right?"

"Right," said Polly. "So?"

"So we swipe Damon's entry form," Denise said. "Without it, he can't enter!"

Polly's eyes widened. "But that would be stealing!"

"Do you want to keep him out or not?" asked Denise.

Polly frowned. She didn't like the idea of stealing. But she didn't have any other ideas.

And if I don't stop Damon, who else will? she said to herself.

"How do we do it?" she asked.

Denise lowered her voice. "Okay, here's the plan . . ."

For the next few days, Polly was busy working on her science project. She'd decided to make a fungus garden from the weird toadstools she found growing in the Kreeps' backyard. She titled her project "What's Fun About Fungi?" and wrote a lot of fungus facts on a big piece of poster board. It turned out really well. Polly thought she might even have a chance of winning the science fair.

Damon was busy, too. Every day after school, he disappeared into his lab, and didn't appear again until morning. At school, he talked nonstop about his project, though he wouldn't tell anyone what it was.

"You have to see it for yourself," he told the other kids. "It's going to be *mind blowing.*"

Soon the whole class was buzzing with talk about Damon's science project. Polly was more worried than ever.

But he's not going to be in the fair, she

reminded herself. *Denise and I are going to make sure of that.*

On the day before the fair, Mr. Crane asked the class to turn in their entry forms. "I can't wait to see the projects you guys have come up with," he said.

The room filled with the sound of shuffling papers as the kids got out their forms and passed them forward. Polly glanced over at Denise, who nodded.

When the stack of forms came to Denise, she suddenly leaped up from her desk, scattering papers across the floor. "A bee!" she shrieked, swatting at the air. "There's a bee in the room!"

The kids sitting near her started to scream, too. "Where is it? A bee! A bee!"

"Calm down, everyone!" Mr. Crane shouted at the class. "Just calm down."

In the commotion, Polly knelt down and collected the spilled papers. She shuffled through them until she found Damon's entry form. The title of his project was "Remote Mind Control."

Polly glanced around to make sure no one was looking, then slid the paper into her desk.

Denise was watching her out of the corner of her eye. As soon as Polly had the form, she sat back down. As Mr. Crane continued to try to control the hysterical class, Denise gave Polly a triumphant wink.

Polly winked back, though she didn't feel triumphant. She still didn't like Denise very much. *At least the plan worked,* she thought.

Polly wondered what her dad or Veronica would say if they knew she'd taken Damon's form. She had a feeling they wouldn't be pleased.

But it's the right thing for everyone, Polly told herself. At least, she hoped it was.

❧ Chapter 8 ❧

The morning of the science fair, Veronica gave the kids a ride to school in her hearse-like station wagon. Esme came, too, riding in the back with Polly's and Damon's science projects. Polly had put her fungus garden in a large cardboard box for the trip to school. Damon's project was in a box, too. He'd written *Top secret — Do not touch* in big black letters on the side.

At school, Mr. Crane gave all the fifth graders time to do last-minute work on their science projects. The fair wouldn't begin for another hour, but everyone was too excited to get any real schoolwork done, anyway.

Even Mr. Crane seemed like he couldn't wait for the fair to start.

"I'm proud to say almost all the fifth graders are participating this year," he told the class. He looked at Damon and his forehead wrinkled. "I have to admit I'm surprised you decided not to enter, Damon. I thought this was the sort of thing you enjoyed."

Damon looked confused. "What do you mean? Of course I'm in the science fair!"

"I didn't get an entry form from you," the teacher pointed out. Polly smiled to herself.

"But I have my project right here!" Damon pointed to the large box beside his desk.

Mr. Crane's face brightened. "Really? That's great, Damon! I knew you wouldn't let the class down. I'll just go down the hall and let Mr. Beaker know we'll have one more student in the fair."

The grin fell off Polly's face, and her hand shot into the air. "But you said everyone had to have an entry form to be in the science fair!" she exclaimed.

"Well, Polly, I'm sure we can make an exception." Mr. Crane smiled. "After all, I'll bet the class wants that ice-cream party."

"Yeah!" the fifth graders said.

Polly couldn't believe it. Damon was getting his way *again*! She stood up from her chair. "It's not fair, Mr. Crane!" she exclaimed. "Rules are rules!"

Mr. Crane looked surprised — and so did the other kids. "Be quiet, Polly!" a few of them hissed. "We want ice cream!"

"Please sit down, Polly," said Mr. Crane.

But Polly wouldn't sit down. "It's not fair!" she repeated, her voice rising. "It's not fair! Rules are rules!"

"Polly, if you don't sit down, I'm going to have to send you to the principal's office," Mr. Crane said, frowning.

"But Mr. Crane, you don't understand —" she began.

"That's it, Polly," the teacher cut her off. "Go see Ms. Stern."

Polly looked around the classroom for someone who would back her up. But she was met with angry glares. Mike looked worried. Denise was casually studying her nails.

"Go on," Mr. Crane told her.

Her heart sinking, Polly turned toward the door. On her way, she caught a glimpse of Damon's face. His evil grin sent a shiver down her spine.

Polly had to wait a long time outside the principal's office. It seemed she wasn't the only one who'd gotten into trouble that day. By the time Polly went in, Ms. Stern looked very tired.

"Don't tell me this has to do with the science fair," she said.

Polly nodded.

Ms. Stern sighed. "Sometimes I think these things are more trouble than they're worth. So let me guess. You spilled your project on the classroom carpet? Set something on fire? Got in a fight with your science partner?"

Polly explained to the principal how Damon had gotten into the science fair without an entry form.

"Well, I'm sure Mr. Crane had a good reason for bending the rules," Ms. Stern said.

"But Damon can't be in the fair. He just can't!" Polly blurted.

Ms. Stern folded her arms on her desk. "Polly, you never got into any trouble at school until your stepbrother started coming here," she said, not unkindly. "Is there some problem between you and Damon? Something happening at home, maybe?"

The problem is that Damon's an evil genius and he's plotting to take over the whole school! Polly thought. But she couldn't say that. She knew the principal would never believe her.

"I'm just worried about Damon's science project," Polly said at last.

"His project? What about it?" Ms. Stern asked.

"I think . . . it could be dangerous," Polly said carefully.

Ms. Stern sat up straighter. "What do you mean?"

"I don't know exactly," Polly admitted. "But I think his project could be bad."

Ms. Stern studied her carefully. "This is very serious, Polly. Are you sure?"

Polly nodded.

"We'd better take care of this at once." Ms. Stern stood up and strode out of her office and down the hall, with Polly scurrying after her.

But when they got to Mr. Crane's room, it was empty. "They must already be in the gym!" said Polly. They turned and raced out of the room.

By the time Polly and the principal got to the gym, the science fair was well underway. Kids and parents milled around, looking at all the different projects. But Polly's attention was drawn to a large knot of people standing near a table at the back of the room. She could see the top of Damon's prickly head just beyond the crowd.

"Oh, no!" Polly gasped. Damon was already there with his project. They were too late!

She hurried through the gym, with Ms. Stern right on her heels. When she neared Damon's table, she saw her dad, Veronica, and Esme standing at the edge of the crowd.

"There you are, Polly!" said Veronica. "We've been looking all over for you, and — what's wrong, dear?" she asked, noticing Polly's face.

"Damon!" Polly gasped. "Where's his project?"

"He's just about to show it to the judges now," Veronica said, nodding at the two teachers who were standing right next to the table. "It's been such a big secret. I can't wait to see what it is."

Polly began trying to push her way through the crowd. "Stop him!" she cried.

But nobody heard. They were all focused on Damon.

"And now, please prepare yourselves for a truly *mind-altering* experience," Damon announced. He whipped away the cloth that was covering his science project. "Behold!"

The crowd leaned forward and peered at the object on the table.

"Hey!" said Polly's dad. "It's the TV remote. I've been looking for that!"

Damon was practically cackling with glee. He picked up the remote control. "This may look like a simple television remote to you. But it is actually a mind-control device — *and now you will all do as I say!*" He raised the remote and hit a button.

"No!" Polly gasped and covered her eyes.

But nothing happened. Polly peeked between her fingers. The crowd was watching Damon with puzzled expressions.

Damon pressed the button again . . . and again. "Dang it! The button is stuck. Wait a second . . . what's this sticky green stuff on it?" He peered closer at the remote.

Polly looked closer, too. The remote seemed to be covered in gunk.

A look of realization crossed Damon's face. He turned to the crowd, eyes blazing. "ESME!"

Esme had handily vanished.

The judges were frowning. "Is this some kind of joke?" asked Ms. Buret.

Mr. Crane shook his head. "Really, Damon," he said. "I expected more of you."

The kids in their class seemed disappointed, too. "Dude," Brad said to Damon, "that was kind of dumb."

"Yeah," added Tad. "I thought you were really going to do something cool." They turned and walked away.

"No, no!" Damon cried, tearing at his hair. "This is all wrong. It wasn't supposed to be like this!"

"Serves you right," Polly heard Veronica say. "What have I told you about world domination, Damon?"

He rolled his eyes. "I know, Mother . . . not until I'm older," he muttered.

"That's right," Veronica said sternly. "Maybe next time you'll listen to me."

Polly smiled to herself. *Ha-ha!* she thought. For once, Damon really was going to get it.

But just then she caught sight of Ms. Stern. The principal's arms were folded and she was frowning at Polly. "Fibbing about dangerous items at school is no laughing matter," she told Polly. "You'll be staying after school every day next week."

As the principal walked away, Polly sighed. It seemed like there was no end to the problems Damon would cause for her.

At that moment, the squeal of a microphone cut through the room. Everyone turned to the front of the room, where the judges were standing. "And now, we'd like to announce the winner of this year's science fair," said Ms. Buret. "First place goes to . . . Mike Willis, for his giant Venus flytrap!"

"Mike?" Polly and Damon exclaimed in unison. They both watched in stunned amazement as Mike collected his prize.

"Bravo, Mike!" exclaimed Veronica, clapping louder than anyone. "Oh, I knew his project was a great idea!"

Oh, well, Polly thought. *Mike deserves it.*

And, she added to herself, *after all, there's always next year.*

Polly's adventures with
the Kreeps continue in

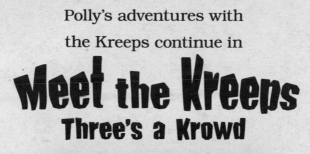

Meet the Kreeps
Three's a Krowd

Turn the page for a sneak
peek . . . if you dare!

Polly Winkler hurried outside to the Endsville Elementary School playground. She'd already missed 15 minutes of recess. She didn't want to waste any more time.

Drat that Damon Kreep, she thought. Somehow, her weird stepbrother had gotten her into trouble again.

Polly's teacher, Mr. Crane, had thought *she* was responsible for the pencil shavings flying around the classroom, when really Polly had only been trying to stop Damon from setting off his newest "scientific" invention. Damon called it a projectile agitator. Polly called it an exploding pencil sharpener. Either way, it had been Polly—not Damon—who'd had to stay indoors, cleaning, for the first half of recess.

Polly liked Mr. Crane. He was all right for a teacher, anyway. When it came to Damon, though, the teacher didn't have a clue. Polly's stepbrother was a ten-year-old mad scientist, with a mind full of sinister schemes and troublesome inventions. But Mr. Crane, as well as the rest of the fifth graders, thought he was just a smart, creative kid. Polly was the only one who knew the truth about Damon and his wacko experiments.

"Polly!" Mike waved from across the playground. He was out on the grass, kicking a soccer ball around with some other kids.

Polly started toward him. But just then a boy kicked the ball to Mike, and he turned away, running toward the goal.

Polly sighed. Mike was busy with his game, and it seemed too late for her to join in. And she didn't want to go anywhere near the basketball court, where Damon was crouched with his best friends, Brad and Tad. What were they up to? Really, Polly didn't want to know.

Just then Polly noticed that the monkey bars were free. That was a surprise. Usually snotty Denise Dunleavy and her follow-along friends got to the monkey bars first. They liked to sit up there all through recess, gossiping and looking down on the rest of the playground.

Polly went over to the bars and pulled herself up. She hooked her knees over a bar so she was hanging upside-down. Then she began to swing her body back and forth, getting ready for a cherry drop.

Polly was mid-swing when someone walked right up to her. From where she was hanging, all Polly could see were two spotless white sneakers. Her gaze traveled up a pair of blue jeans, over a pink T-shirt, and came to rest on the frowning face of Denise Dunleavy.

"Look," Denise said loudly. "There's a

monkey on *our* bars." The two girls with Denise snickered.

Polly took a deep breath. She didn't like Denise, who thought she was better than everyone else just because her parents bought her nice clothes and took her on fancy vacations. Usually when Polly saw Denise coming, she went the other way.

But this time Polly didn't back down. Recess was already half-ruined. Why couldn't she have a turn? After all, Denise didn't own the monkey bars, even if she acted like she did.

"I don't see your name on them," Polly snapped back. She gave her body a hard swing, forcing Denise to step back. Then she flipped off the bars and landed upright, her feet smacking the ground hard.

Denise's frown deepened, and Polly smiled to herself.

But then Denise shrugged and gave a little laugh. "Fine, have it your way. Cherry drops are for babies, anyway."

Denise's friend Misty, who'd been climbing onto the monkey bars, hurriedly got off.

"I'm learning to do a *real* flip on my new trampoline at home," Denise continued. "My parents bought it last week. It's so much fun. *Way* better than this junky old playground equipment. We're also getting a hot tub, you know. Our backyard is huge, so we have plenty of room."

Polly gritted her teeth. She hated to listen to Denise's bragging.

Denise smiled broadly at Polly. "You go ahead and play as long as you like," she said in a sugary voice. "Your house is so small, school is probably the only place where you get to have any fun."

Polly felt her cheeks get red. Ooh! Denise really burned her up! "It just so happens, I live in a mansion," she blurted before she could stop herself.

Denise snorted. "Yeah, right. You're forgetting that I came to your first-grade birthday party, Polly. You live in that little white house on Pleasant Street. I'd hardly call that a mansion."

"That's my old house," Polly snapped. "My *new* house is much bigger. And it has a *swimming pool.*"

The little white house had been Polly's home *before* her dad married Veronica Kreep. After the wedding, her family had moved into the Kreeps' huge, spooky dwelling. Though it was certainly big enough to be called a mansion, the Kreeps' house wasn't exactly glamorous. It had a mossy roof, sagging shutters, and a creaky front door. And although there was a swimming pool, Polly had never put so much in as a toe in its dark, slimy water. But Denise didn't need to know any of that.

Polly was pleased to see a shadow of doubt flicker across Denise's face. She decided to drive home her point.

"Actually, now that I think of it, I'm not sure it's a mansion. It might be a *castle*," Polly told Denise. "It has towers, after all." She decided not to mention that the towers more resembled witches' hats than anything a princess would live in.

Denise narrowed her eyes. "Towers?"

Polly nodded. "Two of them."

Denise tossed her curly brown hair. "I've never heard of a castle in Endsville." She paused, and a sly look slid across her face. "Hey, I know! Why don't we go to your house to play after school today? I've never played in a castle before."

The smile fell from Polly's face. "Er . . . that's not . . . I don't think . . ." she stuttered. What had she done? Denise couldn't come over to her house! If Denise saw where Polly *really* lived, in no time at all everyone at school would know about Polly's freaky family.

Denise took Polly's silence for a yes. "Great. Then it's all settled," she said. "We'll go over to your house — I mean, your *castle* — right after school." Denise snickered. Then, turning on her heel, she flounced away with her friends.

The bell rang, making Polly jump. Recess was over. Polly headed for the school doors, feeling shaky all over. She had to find a way out of this. She had to!

As she started inside, Mike fell into step beside her. "Hey, Polly, you missed a great game —" he began.

"Mike," Polly hissed, pulling him aside. "I need your help! Denise just invited herself over to my house after school! What am I going to do? Once she sees what the Kreeps are really like, she'll tell the whole school. The whole town! My life will be over."

Mike was the only person Polly had told about the Kreeps. He didn't always completely believe Polly, but he was usually on her side. "Maybe it won't be that bad. Just show her the normal parts of the house," he suggested.

"*What* normal part of the house?" she exclaimed. This was going to be a disaster!

Polly blew her bangs out of her eyes. It looked like she was stuck—with Denise and the Kreeps.

Meet the Kreeps

Check out the whole spooky series!

#1: There Goes the Neighborhood

#2: The New Step-Mummy

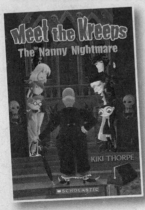

#3: The Nanny Nightmare

#4: The Mad Scientist